OCT 1 5 2019

People Up Close

by Wiley Blevins

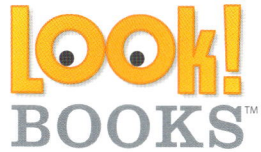

Red Chair Press   Egremont, Massachusetts

Look! Books are produced and published by Red Chair Press:
Red Chair Press LLC   PO Box 333   South Egremont, MA 01258-0333
www.redchairpress.com

 FREE Educator Guides at www.redchairpress.com/free-resources

Publisher's Cataloging-In-Publication Data
Names: Blevins, Wiley.
Title: People up close / by Wiley Blevins.

Description: Egremont, Massachusetts : Red Chair Press, [2019] | Series: Look! books. Look closely | Interest age level: 004-007. | Includes Now You Know fact-boxes, a glossary, and resources for additional reading. | Includes index. | Summary: "In People Up Close, young readers examine portions of several tools-of-the-trade and identify both the tool and the worker who uses it. The reader learns why a hose is a must-have for a firefighter, how a space suit protects an astronaut, what a microscope reveals to a scientist, and how a mixer helps a baker prepare ingredients."--Provided by publisher.

Identifiers: ISBN 9781634406680 (library hardcover) | ISBN 9781634406727 (paperback) | ISBN 9781634406765 (ebook)

Subjects: LCSH: Occupations--Juvenile literature. | Equipment and supplies--Juvenile literature. | Tools--Juvenile literature. | CYAC: Occupations. | Tools.

Classification: LCC HF5381.2 .B54 2019 (print) | LCC HF5381.2 (ebook) | DDC 331.702 [E]--dc23

LCCN: 2018955659

Copyright © 2020 Red Chair Press LLC
RED CHAIR PRESS, the RED CHAIR and associated logos are registered trademarks of Red Chair Press LLC.

All rights reserved. No part of this book may be reproduced, stored in an information or retrieval system, or transmitted in any form by any means, electronic, mechanical including photocopying, recording, or otherwise without the prior written permission from the Publisher. For permissions, contact info@redchairpress.com

Photo credits: pp. 1–13, 14, 16–17, 18, 20, 24 Shutterstock; cover, pp. 15, 19, 21–22 iStock.

Printed in United States of America

0519 1P CGF19

Table of Contents

I'm All Wet.......................... 4

Out of This World 8

Mini Me 12

One Big Mix-Up 16

Test Yourself! 20

Words to Keep 23

Learn More at the Library 23

Index.............................24

I'm All Wet

It's long. It can curl up like a snake. Open a **valve** and *WHOOSH!* What is it? And who uses it?

It's a water hose. A firefighter uses it. *Zoom!* A fire truck races to the burning building. The firefighter points the water hose. The water helps put out the fire!

GOOD to KNOW

If you see a fire, call 9-1-1. To get out of your house, STOP, DROP, and ROLL.

Out of This World

This is mostly white. It can be hard or soft. It's worn over the worker's clothes. It keeps the worker **safe**. What is it? And who uses it?

It's a space suit. An astronaut wears it. It keeps the astronaut warm in outer space. This suit makes sure the astronaut has air to breathe, too.

GOOD to KNOW

Sally Ride became the first American female astronaut in 1983.

In July 1969 a human walked on the moon for the very first time.

Mini Me

This tool makes **tiny** things look very big. The worker looks inside. Wow! A new world comes into view. What is it? And who uses it?

It's a microscope. A scientist uses it. The scientist **investigates** things too small to see with just your eyes. Everything looks different under a microscope.

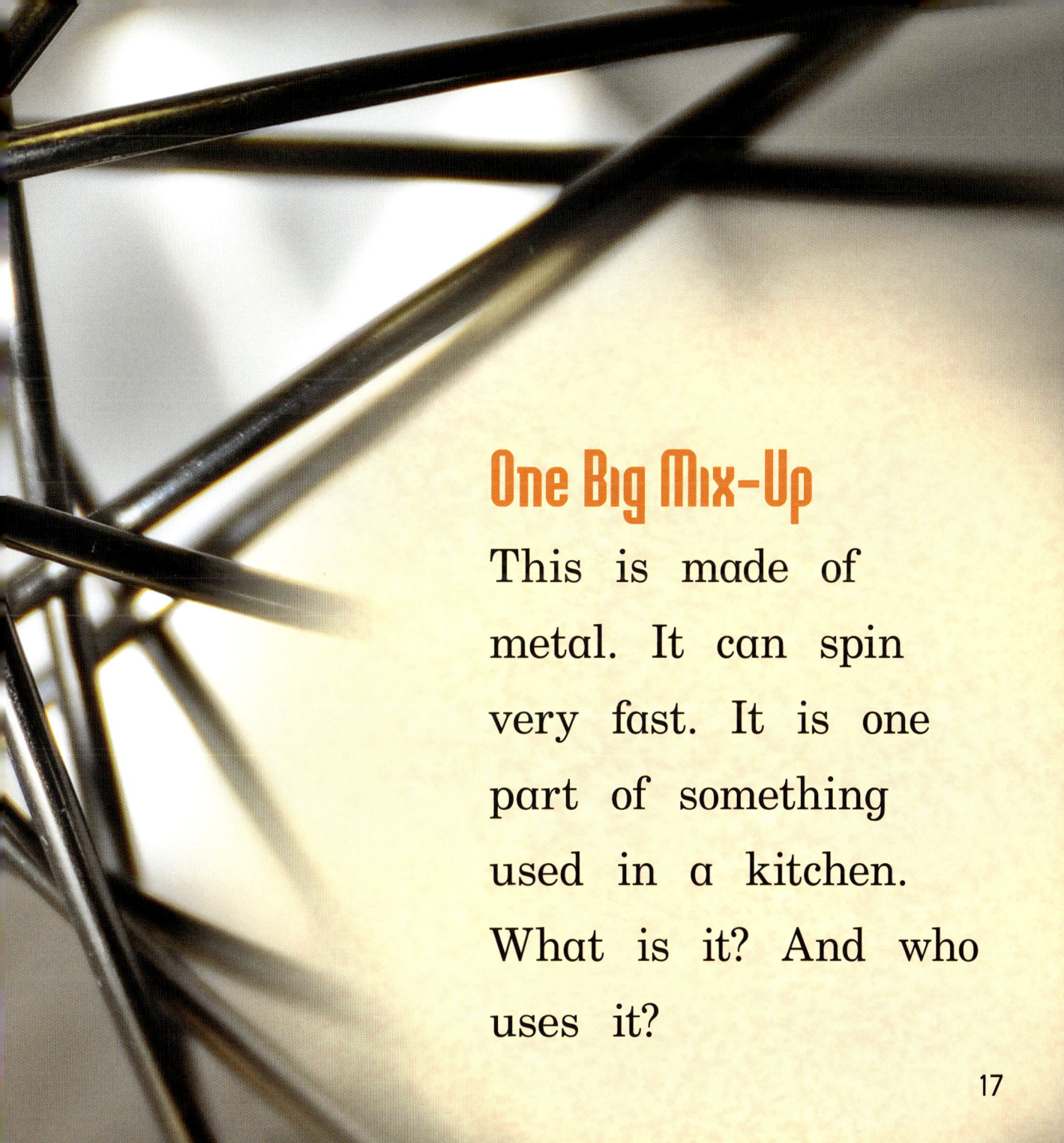

One Big Mix-Up

This is made of metal. It can spin very fast. It is one part of something used in a kitchen. What is it? And who uses it?

It's the beater for a mixer. A baker uses it to mix **ingredients**. The ingredients go into a pan. Then the pan goes into the oven. Soon the cake will be done. *Yum!*

Test Yourself!

What are these things? Who uses each one? There are no clues. But you may have seen them all. Look closely!

1. clown
2. ballet dancer
3. crossing guard

Words to Keep

ingredients: parts of a mixture, like eggs and flour

investigate: to study or look closely at something

safe: free from danger or harm

tiny: very small

valve: something that controls the flow of water through a pipe or hose

Learn More at the Library

Books (Check out these books to learn more.)

Hayward, Linda. *A Day in the Life of a Firefighter.* DK Readers, 2001.

Huff, Lisa. *Kid Chef Bakes.* Rockridge Press, 2017.

Rustad, Martha E. H. *Working in Space.* Capstone Press, 2018.

Web sites (Ask an adult to show you these web sites.)

Stop, Drop, and Roll
https://www.youtube.com/watch?v=aUdxOmHgeZ4

I Want to Be an Astronaut
https://www.youtube.com/watch?v=vbKixwY95pg

Index

astronaut 9–10
baker 18–19
firefighter 6–7
microscope 12–15
mixer beater 16–19
scientist 14–15
space suit 8–11
water hose 4–7

About the Author

Wiley Blevins has written many books for kids. Wiley uses a computer to write his books.